Chester the BRAVE

By Audrey Penn

Illustrated by Barbara L. Gibson

Tanglewood • Terre Haute, IN

Published by Tanglewood Publishing, Inc., October, 2012
Text © 2012 Audrey Penn
Illustrations © 2012 Barbara L. Gibson

Design by Amy Alick Perich

Tanglewood Publishing, Inc.
4400 Hulman St.
Terre Haute, IN 47803
www.tanglewoodbooks.com

Printed in U. S. A.
10 9 8 7 6 5 4 3 2 1

ISBN 1-933718-79-X
ISBN 978-1-933718-79-8

Library of Congress Cataloging-in-Publication Data

Penn, Audrey, 1947-
  Chester the brave / Audrey Penn, author ; Barbara L. Gibson, illustrator.
    p. cm.
  Summary: A young raccoon learns the meaning of bravery and a method for overcoming his fears.
  ISBN 1-933718-79-X (978-1-933718-79-8)
  [1. Fear--Fiction. 2. Courage--Fiction. 3. Raccoon--Fiction.] I. Gibson, Barbara, ill. II. Title.
  PZ7.P38448Ck 2012
  [E]--dc23
                        2012008401

For Cale and Ila and Jude
-AP

Thank you to Daniella, Mathew, Ryan, and Rebecca for listening to my story and telling me how to fix it. The changes make it much better.
Love, Aunt Audrey

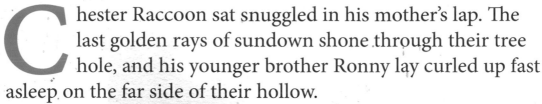

Chester Raccoon sat snuggled in his mother's lap. The last golden rays of sundown shone through their tree hole, and his younger brother Ronny lay curled up fast asleep on the far side of their hollow.

"This is my very best time," Chester told his mother, lifting his eyes to hers.

"This is my very best time, too," she told him sweetly. "Do you still want me to tell you about the little robin?"

"Yes, please."

"Well," Mrs. Raccoon began her story. "He stepped up to the edge of his nest, bent his little legs, lifted his tiny wings, and said, 'I can't. I'm too afraid,' and hopped back into the safety of his nest."

"He was too afraid to fly?" asked Chester.

"Yes, he was," answered Mrs. Raccoon.

Chester looked very worried. He drooped his head and stuck out his lower lip. "Did the little robin think it was okay to be afraid?"

"He thought it meant he wasn't brave," explained Chester's mother. "You see, the little robin's brother and sister flew their very first time, and he thought that meant they were very brave. And if they were very brave, he thought it meant he wasn't."

Chester appeared very upset. "Was he right?" he asked his mother.

Mrs. Raccoon smoothed out the fur on top of Chester's head. "Well, the little robin's father told him that it wasn't that his brother and sister were brave, it was the fact that they simply weren't bothered."

Chester lifted his head and peered up at his mother. "What does that mean?"

Mrs. Raccoon laughed. "The little robin wasn't sure what it meant either, so his father asked him if he was bothered when he was eating worms."

"Ooh, yuck!" shrieked Chester. "That's disgusting! What did he say?"

"He said he wasn't bothered eating worms at all. He said he loved eating worms—especially the big, long, thick, stretchy kind!"

"Oh! Blech!" bleated Chester. His nose and mouth twisted and squished together, and his entire body shuddered. "Eating worms would bother me."

Mrs. Raccoon nodded. "It would bother me, too," she confessed. "Then the little robin's father asked him if he was bothered when he was singing, and the little birdie began tweeting and said he wasn't bothered when he was singing at all!"

"Singing is a lot better than eating worms," grimaced Chester.
"I agree," said Mrs. Raccoon. "Then, the little bird's father
told him that being brave wasn't about flying when he wasn't
bothered to fly. Being brave was about flying when he was
bothered to fly but found the courage to fly anyway because
he knew he must.

"Then his father asked him if he was bothered when he was reciting his flying lessons in front of all the other little birdies who nested in our tree. The poor little robin got all aflutter.

He hopped up and down and flapped his wings, just like he did the time the skunk sprayed our tree from down below. The little robin said that reciting his lessons in front of all the other little birds was the worst thing he ever had to do in his whole life!"

Suddenly Chester began to tremble, and he nestled deeper into his mother's soft, comforting arms.

"What's the matter?" his mother asked.

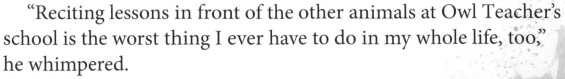

"Reciting lessons in front of the other animals at Owl Teacher's school is the worst thing I ever have to do in my whole life, too," he whimpered.

"Is that so?" asked Mrs. Raccoon. She gave Chester a reassuring hug and then took his tiny hand in hers and gently kissed the center of his palm. "Shall I tell you what happened to the little robin, or would you rather jump on top of Ronny and wake him up for school?"

Chester giggled. "I want to know what happened to the robin."

"Well, the very next day, the little robin's mother tucked one of her own tiny flight feathers into his wing and told him it was for good luck.

"So even though he was still bothered about reciting his lessons, the tiny bird stood in front of all the other birdies in our tree and twittered, 'I lift my head to the clouds. I push off with my feet. I flap my wings and let the gentle breeze take me for a ride.'

And while he was still afraid to fly, he found the courage he needed and said to himself, 'I am very brave.'

"Then he stepped up to the edge of his nest, spread his wings, pushed off with his feet, and flew away. After all, he was a very brave little robin."

"Hurray!" clapped Chester.

"Do you know what I think being brave is?" asked Mrs. Raccoon.

Chester shook his head.

"I think being brave is about three little words: **Think—Tell—Do.** If you **think** you can't, **tell** yourself you can, and **do** it!" Mrs. Raccoon lifted Chester's hand. "Can you see my kiss in your palm?"

Chester laughed. "No."

"Well, you know it's there. And it's for luck, just like the robin's little feather."

Chester jumped off his mother's lap, bent his knees, opened his arms, and yelled, "I am very brave!" Then he ran to the other side of the hollow and, with a flying leap, landed on top of his brother.

"Wake up, Ronny. It's time for school! Chester the Brave has a speech to make."

Later that night, Chester Raccoon stood on a branch at Owl Teacher's school. He remembered what his mother said about **Think—Tell—Do**.

"If I **think** I can't, I **tell** myself I can and **do** it!" And he found the courage he needed to tell himself, "I am very brave." Then he opened his hand, and there, in the middle of his palm, was his mother's gentle kiss for good luck.

And even though Chester was still the tiniest bit afraid, he recited his lesson in front of all the other animals.

After all, Chester is a very brave little raccoon.